This book belongs to

....

For my Mum and Dad and sister Mandi
who always believed in me. And for Dave
who made me believe in myself.

ISBN 978-1-84135-912-0

Copyright © Laura Wall

First published 2012

Published by Award Publications Limited,
The Old Riding School, The Welbeck Estate,
Worksop, Nottinghamshire, S80 3LR

www.awardpublications.co.uk

13 3

Printed in China

Also available:
Goose Goes to School
Goose Goes to the Zoo
Happy Birthday, Goose!
Goose on the Farm
Goose Goes Shopping

Goose

by Laura Wall

AWARD PUBLICATIONS LIMITED

This is Sophie.

She likes to play with her dolls.

And dress up.

But this isn't much fun on her own.

Sophie's mum takes her to the park.

Sophie wants to go on the see-saw.

But someone else is already playing on it.

So instead she sits on the slide.

And swings on the swings.

Sophie wishes she had a
friend to play with.

But wait. What's that?

The goose follows Sophie.

They play on the see-saw.

And on the slide.

And they swing on the swings.

When it is time to go home
Goose wants to come, too.

But Mum says no.

"Goodbye, Goose!"

The next day Sophie goes back to the park.

And who should be there but Goose!

They play on the see-saw again.

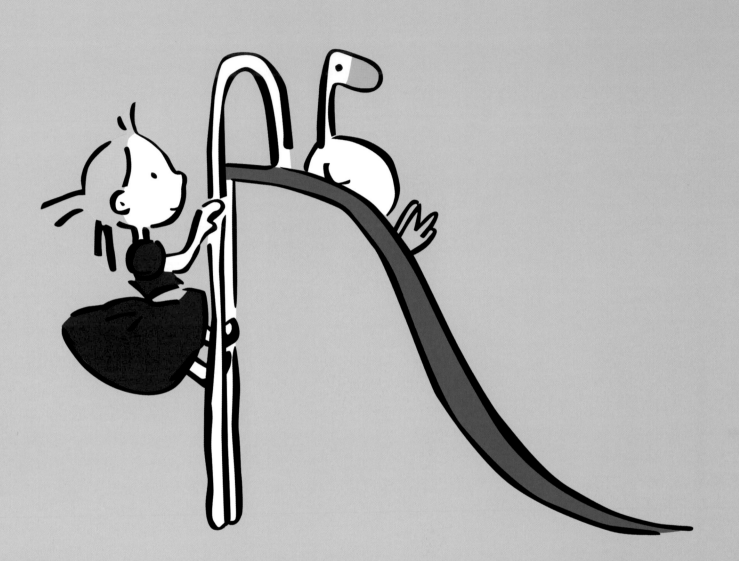

And on the slide.

And they swing on the swings.

Then Goose looks sad.

His friends are flying away for the winter.
It is time for him to go.

"Goodbye, Goose!"

The next day Sophie goes to the park again.

But Goose is not there.

Nothing is quite as much fun.

Not without Goose.

But when it is time to go home,
Sophie hears a familiar sound.

Honk!

"Goose! You came back!"

"Please can Goose come home?"

"OK," says Mum.
"If he promises to be good."

"Honk!" says Goose.